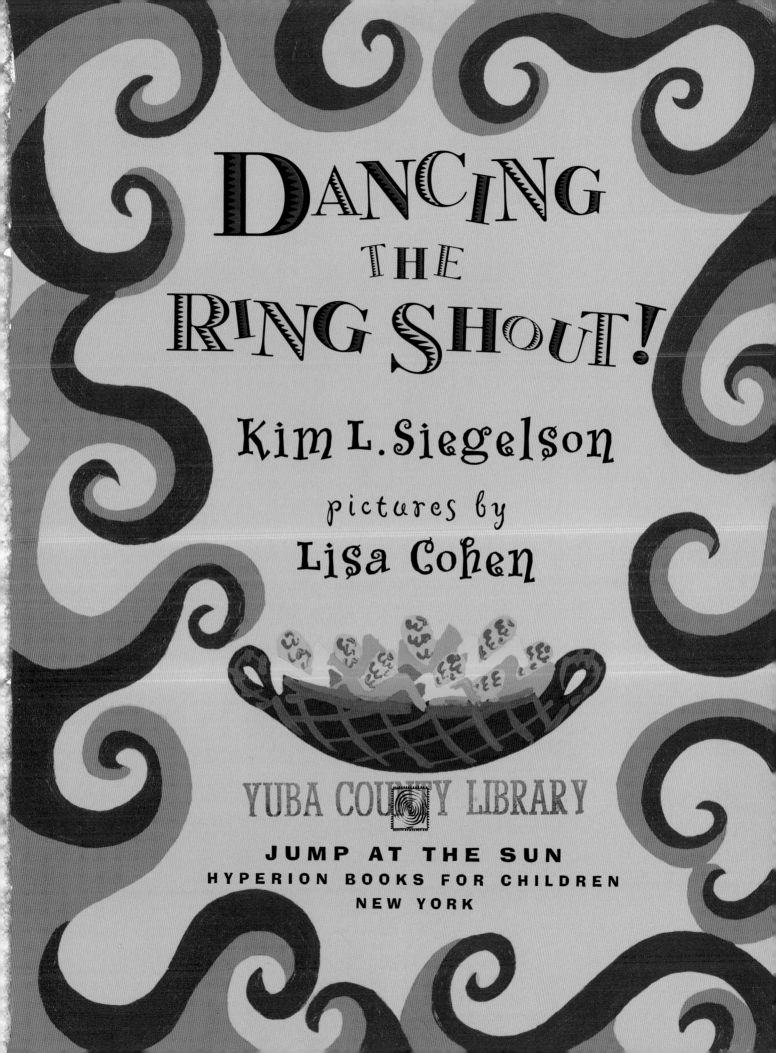

DanCing the RinG Shout!

Kim L. Siegelson

pictures by
Lisa Cohen

JUMP AT THE SUN
HYPERION BOOKS FOR CHILDREN
NEW YORK

SELECTED SOURCES

Down Yonder—The MacIntosh County Shouters. Documentary
Film. Produced by Clate Sanders. Georgia Public Television, 1987.

Parrish, Lydia. *Slave Songs of the Georgia Sea Islands* (1942).
Reprinted in 1992 with foreword by Art Rosenbaum. Athens, Ga.:
University of Georgia Press.

Raboteau, Albert J. *Slave Religion: The "Invisible Institution" in the
Antebellum South.* Oxford: Oxford University Press, 1978.

Rosenbaum, Art. *The MacIntosh County Singers: Slave Shout Songs
from the Coast of Georgia.* New York: Ethnic Folkways Records, 1984.

Rosenbaum, Art, and Margo Newmark Rosenbaum. *Shout Because
You're Free: The African American Ring Shout Tradition in Coastal
Georgia.* Athens, Ga.: University of Georgia Press, 1998.

For my parents, and all who
"shout unto God with the voice of triumph"
(Psalm 47:1)

—K.L.S.

For Chicken, Seb, Buttercup, and Goosey

—L.C.

ON THE LAST DAY of the harvest year, the sun rose fat and warm as a hoecake over Appling Farm. Pearl and Mam shelled dry beans into burlap sacks. Toby passed each one to Grand to stitch closed. "Come moon-up we'll ring-shout," Grand said. "And this year Toby is old enough to take his place in the circle."

Grand pulled the thread up tight and snapped it between his teeth. "You must bring something with you to play along with the singing, Toby."

"What can I bring?" Toby asked.

"Something that speaks from your heart straight to the ears of God," Grand answered, and tied a knot in the thread. He patted the head of his walking stick.

"I always bring my cane. When I pound it on the ground, it sounds like the hooves of our plow mule that breaks dirt open in spring. I give praise for our mule."

Grand had a cane. Toby wondered what he could bring that would speak from his own heart to God's ears.

Outside the barn Toby helped Pap shovel corn into the cribs. Crows cawed back and forth like old friends. Pap took off his hat to wipe the salt from his brow. "Come moon-up we'll ring-shout. It won't be long."

Toby wiped his own brow like a man. "What will you bring to play along with the music, Pap?"

Pap smiled. "My hoop drum, same as last year. It booms like the thunderclouds that bring rain to our crops. I am thankful for the rain."

Pap had his hoop drum;
Grand had a cane.
What could Toby
bring that would
speak from his
own heart to
God's ears?

In the kitchen Toby watched
Mam roll out dinner biscuits
on the counter.

"What will you bring to the ring shout, Mam?" Toby asked.

Mam plopped the biscuits into a baking pan. "I am bringing two tin pans. They clang like the hoe blades that clear the weeds from the rows in our field. I am grateful for them."

Mam had tin pans; Pap had his hoop drum; Grand had his cane. What could Toby bring that would speak from his own heart to God's ears?

Toby played checkers on the back steps with Pearl. "What are you bringing to the ring shout?" he asked her.

Pearl jumped two of his checkers. "I'm bringing a dry gourd. The seeds inside rattle like cornstalks in the wind. I am happy for the wind on hot days."

Pearl had a gourd;

Mam had tin pans;

Pap had his hoop drum;

Grand had his cane.

What could Toby bring that would
speak from his own heart to God's ears?

Toby found two sticks under the pecan tree and tapped them together. **RAP, TAPA, TAP!**

His heart did not speak.

Toby tried jangling a cowbell in the shed. **CLANG, CLONG, CLANK!** His heart did not speak.

Toby rubbed two stiff horse brushes together. **Shoo, swish, shush!** His heart still did not speak.

Soon the autumn moon hung pumpkin-round
above the farm, and Toby had not found
the one special thing that would speak
from his heart to the ears of God.
Slow as molasses syrup,
he went to tell Grand.

"My hands are empty," he said. "I don't have anything to take to the ring shout tonight, so I'm not going."

Grand's dark eyes twinkled in the moonglow. He pointed at the empty fields. "Way back in the slave time, our people came to this land with nothing in their hands. Every day they planted and grew and tended what they could not keep. Even so, they danced each harvesttime because the hard work was done. With empty hands their hearts still spoke to God.

Yours will, too."

Toby stared out over Appling Farm.
His heart felt as empty and quiet as the fields.

Out at the meeting place fire sparks swirled above the treetops like stars shooting across the heavens. Some folks began to sing a hymn, while others started a sliding step that stirred up dust till it looked like clouds of smoke.

Grand banged his cane in time, and Pap beat his drum. Mam clanged her tin pans and Pearl shook her gourd like the roaring wind.

Toby stood empty-handed outside the circle.

The dancers moved faster, around and around, and the voices rose louder.

They called out:
"Grateful for corn!
Grateful for beans!
Happy for gourds!
Happy for peas!
We give thanks for our harvest,
For hard work and rest; raise up our arms

**SHOUT
WE ARE BLESSED!"**

Toby could feel the song and the dance all the way to his insides. His bones hummed and his heart beat like Pap's drum. Suddenly he brought his empty hands together.

CLAP! CLAP! CLAP!

He joined the circle and swayed and stomped until he thought his heart would burst.

Toby danced the ring shout all night until his palms turned red as the sunrise.

When the sky turned as pale as buttermilk, the ring shout ended for another year.

"Did you speak with your heart?" Grand asked Toby on the long walk home.

"No, sir," he answered. "I spoke with everything I had, from my toes to my nose."

Grand cackled like the crows. "You must be mighty thankful for something, then."

"I am," Toby said, and slipped his empty hand inside Grand's.